Beach Is

A Book of Relationships

Henry Holt and Company • New York

to Fun

by Pat Brisson

illustrated by Sachiko Yoshikawa

Henry Holt and Company, LLC
Publishers since 1866
115 West 18th Street
New York, New York 10011
www.henryholt.com

Henry Holt is a registered trademark of Henry Holt and Company, LLC
Text copyright © 2004 by Pat Brisson
Illustrations copyright © 2004 by Sachiko Yoshikawa
Distributed in Canada by H. B. Fenn and Company Ltd.

Library of Congress Cataloging-in-Publication Data
Brisson, Pat.
Beach is to fun: a book of relationships / Pat Brisson; illustrated by Sachiko Yoshikawa.
Summary: A day at the beach is the occasion for this rhyming look at the relationships between things.
[1. Beaches—Fiction. 2. English language—Analogy. 3. Stories in rhyme.]
I. Yoshikawa, Sachiko, ill. II. Title.
PZ8.3.B7745Be 2004   [E]—dc21   2003002619

ISBN 0-8050-7315-9 / First Edition—2004
Designed by Martha Rago
Printed in the United States of America on acid-free paper. ∞
1 3 5 7 9 10 8 6 4 2
The artist used acrylic and pastel on watercolor paper to create the illustrations for this book.

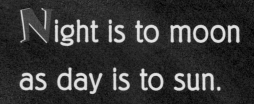

Night is to moon
as day is to sun.

School is to work
as beach is to fun.

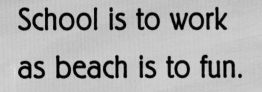

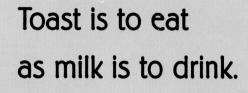

Toast is to eat
as milk is to drink.

Voice is to talk
as mind is to think.

Path is to bike
as street is to car.

Back is to front
as near is to far.

Red is to green
as stop is to go.

On is to off
as yes is to no.

Sun is to yellow
as cloud is to white.

Up is to down
as left is to right.

Gull is to sky
as shell is to sand.

Child is to family
as finger is to hand.

Sea is to salty
as candy is to sweet.

Hat is to head
as sandals are to feet.

Winter is to cold
as summer is to hot.

Little is to big

as rowboat is to yacht.

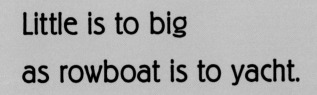

Ball is to hit
as disc is to throw.

Toss is to catch
as fast is to slow.

I am to land
as crab is to sea.

Claws are to crab
as hands are to me.

Water is to wet
as towel is to dry.

Arm is to swim
as wing is to fly.

Juice is to cup
as water is to pail.

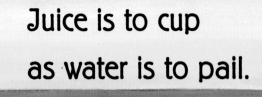

Raft is to float
as boat is to sail.

Knight is to castle
as small is to large.

Road is to wagon
as ocean is to barge.

at the beach

Grains are to beach
as drops are to sea.

Gramps is to Dad
as Dad is to me.

fishing

Sleep is to dark
as play is to light.

Beach is to day
as home is to night.